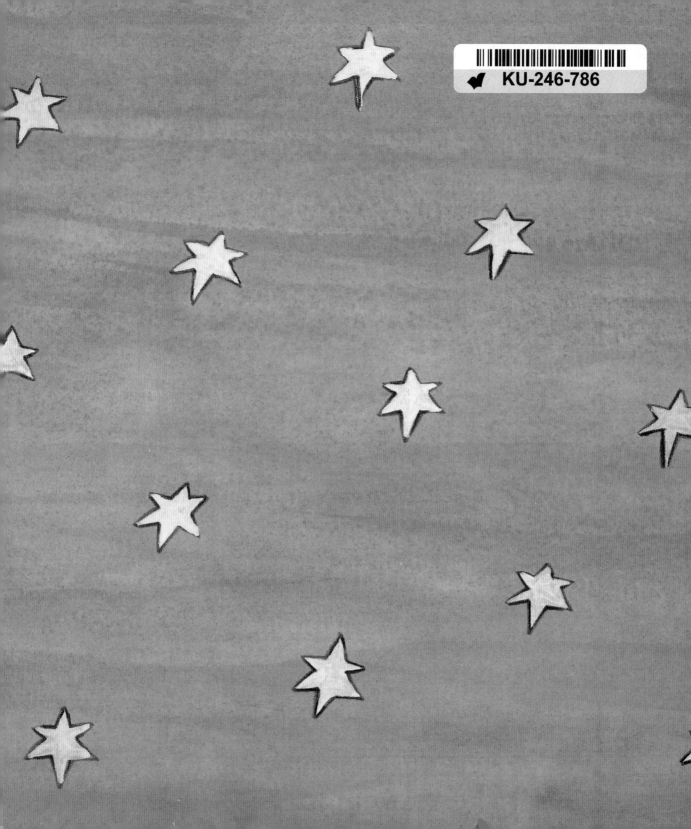

For Eloise Lily Maltby Maland,
with love – S. J-P.

MYRIAD BOOKS LIMITED
35 Bishopsthorpe Road, London SE26 4PA

First published in 1996 by
FRANCES LINCOLN LIMITED
4 Torriano Mews
Torriano Avenue
London NW5 2RZ

ISBN 1 84746 047 X
EAN 9 781 84746 047 9

Printed in China

ANNIE ANGEL

Susie Jenkin-Pearce

MYRIAD BOOKS LIMITED

Annie's grandma bought her angel wings for Christmas.

They were the best present of all.

Annie wore them all the time. She NEVER took them off!

"Annie's no angel," said Dad as he tucked
her up in bed. "Only Grandma thinks so."

Annie wanted to wear her wings to school,
but Mum said, "NO!" So Annie told Lucy
about her wings on the way.

The new topic at school was flight.
"We'll have a show at the end of term,"
said Miss Sally, their teacher.

"I have angel wings," said Annie. "Angels fly.
I could be an angel in the show."

"Mmm... How about being an aeroplane?" smiled her teacher.

But Annie wanted to be an angel. She picked
flowers for Miss Sally on the way to school.

She cleaned out the mouse.

She washed up the paint pots.

She tidied the books.

"Oh no, Annie!" gasped Miss Sally. "No more help, PLEASE."

Poor Annie. If only she did things right, like Lucy.

That night, Annie dreamed of angels.

She dreamed of flying about doing
kind things that DIDN'T go wrong.

But it was only a dream. Next morning, Annie carefully carried her wings to school.

"Lucy can wear these," she said. "She'll make the best angel."
"But Annie," said Miss Sally, "your wings were your special
present. Are you sure?"

Annie nodded and Miss Sally smiled.
"You wear them," she said. "Perhaps you'll
make a perfect angel after all."

And she did…